The Ruling Elite and Other Stories

The Ruling Elite and Other Stories

Xina Marie Uhl and Janet Loftis

XC Publishing.net

BISAC subject headings:

FIC009040   FICTION / Fantasy / Collections & Anthologies

FIC009070   FICTION / Fantasy / Dark Fantasy

FIC009030   FICTION / Fantasy / Historical

XC Publishing
653 Calle Pensamiento
Thousand Oaks, CA 91360
www.XCPublishing.net

Contents

Part I

Where fantasy meets history

The stories of Xina Marie Uhl

The Ruling Elite

Wind swept off the frozen ridge, worming its way around the leather armor-collar at my neck and the rags tied around my red, chafed hands. I scarcely felt the knife in my grasp. I only prayed that when the time came I would have enough mobility left to save our lives.

Halis lay where she had collapsed, her skin as pale as the hard-packed ice around us; dark hair and dark rings around her eyes making the contrast more striking. Her breath came short and shallow, a hoarse rattling sounded somewhere deep in her chest. I had never seen her so ill. I wasn't sure she would live even if I did manage to fight off the Ulbari.

Kneeling next to her, I undid the folds of her garments to make sure her wound wasn't festering. Sweat beaded my forehead and clotted my underarms. My fingers trembled. I thought of my mother, a tavern whore in the streets of Netria: caressing my hair, kissing my cheek, laughing with her customers behind beaded curtains. My dark-haired, beautiful mother, screaming in agony as she gave in to one of the fits of madness that had dogged her periodically throughout my childhood, and flung herself off a bridge in the old section of town. I clamped the memory off.

The wound was ragged and deep, a red and purple mass of torn tissue. As was the custom of the healers, I left it unbandaged to drain. If there had been time for rest, proper food, and the healing balms of the city, Halis would have had a good chance at recovering.

Roused by my probing, her eyelids flickered open. She placed cold fingers on my arm.

"Have they found us?"

"No."

"Good, I'll sleep."

"No. We must move. Get up."

She closed her eyes again, gave a sigh that frosted the air. "Leave me be."

"I can't. You know that."

"If you cared about me you would."

I looked away, over the snowy fields. I don't care for you, I thought. I never will.

"Please, I just need to sleep for a little while . . . "

Her eyes closed and her breathing deepened--sleeping, despite my orders. Three years ago she had bought me from the mercenary troop I had sworn my honor to. She had never sold her honor like I had; perhaps that is why she ignored me.

Our journey had begun as a caravan of twenty-three men and seven women pledged to escort Halis to the holy city of Samarra. There, she was to discharge her obligation to her patron goddess Korei. Halis's family had many enemies, so I chose experienced soldiers to accompany us, and planned our route carefully. But in the end it was all useless. The Ulbari had ambushed us as we traveled through the ice fields between Samarra and Kabala. I fought as well as I could, but our party was outnumbered and the Ulbari were renowned mercenaries.

Halis had never held a weapon in her whole pampered life, but when one of the Ulbari rushed her and her attendants, she picked up a fallen spear and stuck him in the thigh. The blow didn't stop him and by the time I reached her, the Ulbari had stabbed her in the chest. I killed him, but others kept coming and those I could not stop. Securing Halis in one arm and slashing back and forth like a reaper with the other, I fought free of the fracas. I wanted to stay, but I was bodyguard to Halis, so I let the deaths of the others mask our escape across the snow.

The code of my Company governed my life: protect, honor and serve your master, die for him, or if you can, die with him, and always defend the code of Kuba, god of peace and war. But when we left the others to die I hated Halis for who she was—Elan, the ruling elite. And more, Dela-Elan, elite of the elite. My class was forever dying for hers.

*

When Halis woke, our journey began again. I half-carried her across the endless white snow, now and then slipping, more frequently resting. She seemed to grow heavier with each step.

The brightness of the sun hurt my eyes, but I turned my face to it to glean every bit of warmth. The world was made of ice--jutting half-walls, fractured mountains and smooth veinless marble all jumbled together, without patterns. Here, wind and sleet and sun were the only forces and chance the only god.

After a while I ceased being cold. The white fields reminded me of home, with its long white beaches and blue sky and the surf rolling unendingly against the sands.

[5]

Halis moved like a sleepwalker, eyes glazed and gait stilted. Once she stopped, squinting against the glaring white snow as though seeing the ice fields for the first time.

"The Ulbari are still following us?"

I looked back over the white hills, saw nothing. "Yes."

She fixed her gaze on me and cocked her head inquiringly. "Where are we going?"

"The sea." The settlements in this inhospitable land lay primarily along the coast, and I knew that if we made it there we would be able to find one without too much trouble.

A slight smile brushed across her lips and she resumed walking, on ahead of me.

The Elanian priests called the sea healer and life-giver, harborer of food and mystery, watery birthplace of the gods. Mother to us all. But to me the sea was a cold place, distant and uncaring, remote and dangerous.

*

We stopped that night in a small damp cave perched halfway up a rocky hill. Halis barely slept, tortured by intense cold and the pain of her wound. I did not sleep at all, but instead watched the moon make her silvery trek across the night sky. I could not see any sign of the Ulbari, but I knew they were out there, lurking at the edge of the world.

Halis tossed and turned and moaned, finding nothing but snatches of fitful sleep. Finally she crawled over to me and lay her head in my lap.

I stared down at her for a long moment, surprised at this unexpected intimacy. But she seemed beyond the pride of class restrictions in her weariness and pain.

I had been angry with her for as long as I could remember. She who made me follow her around like a trained puppy, remaining silent as she called me a donkey because of my silence, dragging me to all the places the cursed Dela-Elan frequented--the lecture halls and marketplaces and long, drunken festivals. I despised the easy duty, the long boring days. But I did not complain. Anything was better than the times before the guard.

The only thing I had truly liked about Halis was her vitality, which seemed to glow like a bright white flame from within her. That vitality made her more beautiful than her exquisite eyes or long hair or smooth skin. But here, in this white, cold place, I could feel even that slipping away, hour by hour. Moment by moment.

It had been three days since we'd escaped the Ulibari, and in that time the only thing we'd had to eat was a strip of dried meat I'd kept with my pack. At dawn I left, searching the frozen fields for game or roots to fill our shrunken bellies. I found nothing but a still, dead, silent world.

Trudging back to Halis, I ignored the aches and pains and lightheaded weariness dogging my steps.

She had dragged herself to a sunny spot outside the cave and lay with her head on our packs, looking impassively at the terrain ahead.

"Come. The sea awaits," I told her.

She looked paler today; even her lips, once red as rose petals, were bleached of color. In a curiously dead tone, she said, "I'll never reach the sea. Leave me here to die."

I sighed. "No, lady."

She stared directly into my eyes. Her own possessed flecks of gold I had never noticed before. "Listen to me. You know I don't speak idly."

"I can't leave you."

"You can," she said softly. "Your obligation to me is fulfilled. Go settle in some seaside town and raise a family."

Her words struck me like a baton in the stomach. I would be with her until my death. I was an initiate of Kuba, god of war. At thirteen years of age I had taken the mantle of the soldier across my shoulders; nothing remained of the time before that but a handful of nightmares. I had never known my father and my mother died when I was seven, leaving me to beg in the streets for crusts of bread, alone and scared, wearing rags and shivering from cold and sickness in wattle and dung huts.

Life began again when I sold myself to the mercenary troop. I was clean and fed and strong. I followed the dictates of my commander, fought when I was told to, slept when I could and got drunk in the meantime. None of the men had families, though some had concubines or whores or even each other. I preferred to be by myself. Never before had I considered giving up my life for a family, like one of the old freed slaves, smoking hashish as grandchildren played at their knees.

"I cannot," I told her.

A shadow of a smile crossed her lips. "Even donkeys have mates and offspring."

"I have duty." It was all I needed.

*

We followed the sunlight until the hard-packed snow had hardened into ice. Halis had grown so weak that I supported her almost exclusively now, though I suspected that my bumping, jostling, and occasional slip on the slick ice made her even more miserable.

I charted our progress by the sun; it was the only thing alive here. Our path took us through a stretch of low, rolling hills that made our trek even more slippery. After a while, I decided to double back and make our way around the hills instead of through them. We had gone no more than half a mile when we heard low voices just around the next bend. The Ulbari.

Halis and I froze in place, barely breathing. We listened again for the voices in the hopes that we had heard nothing but the whisper of the wind. They came again. Halis turned around slowly, so that her gaze met mine.

I will remember her expression all of my days: wide-eyed, tight-lipped, blanched with fear. Her fingers dug into my arms. In a strained, barely audible voice, she whispered, "Don't fight them. Let's just keep running."

"You can barely walk, much less run."

"Then leave me here; let them kill me and save yourself." Her eyes filled with desperation bordering on madness.

I shook free of her grasp. "Stop talking like this. I must perform my duty."

The passion and terror she had displayed moments past drained from her face. Wearily, she said, "Of course. You always do."

And then I was off and running up the side of a small rise. At the top, I crouched and watched our foes. Two of them, talking in low tones and gesturing at the ground. Trying to decide which way to go, I assumed. One of them looked around suddenly, as if he had heard a noise, and I saw the brown flatness of his face and the thick bushy eyebrows beetling over dark eyes. Then he turned back and I knew that he had not seen me. Felt that I was here, perhaps, but then disregarded that notion. Too bad for him.

The surprise on the Ulbari's faces was almost comical as I flew off the rise and collided with the smaller of the two. We landed hard on the packed ice, my opponent on the bottom. The breath knocked out of him, he nonetheless scrambled away from me, pawing at his furs for the long-handled pike that was the barbarians' favorite weapon.

Battle-madness crested over in me. I felt nothing but the high of the moment, heart hammering and muscles working and the cool, fresh breath tearing in and out of my lungs. Life never felt so clear and bright and precious as when I was in danger of losing it.

I killed quickly. The Ulbari, clumsy in his surprise and panic, fumbled his pike to the ground. I snatched it and stuck him in the neck. Blood splashed across the snow in a perfect, dark red arc.

From behind, the other Ulbari collided with me, breaking ribs with the impact. Pain blinded me, then passed. I had never allowed pain or injury to overpower me in the heat of battle; I simply ignored them and fought on.

[10]

Springing to my feet, I pulled my dagger free in one fluid motion. The Ulbari's eyes were wild and sweat beaded his forehead despite the cold. With a low growl, he rushed me. We rolled around on the snow, grasping and grabbing and smashing each other in the face, gut, and loins. From his belt, he produced a jikar, a silver spike that fit around the back of his hand. I countered with my serrated dagger. He tried to use his bigger bulk to trap me and pierce my throat; I stabbed him in the side and slashed his cheek to the bone. As I pulled away, he lunged at me with his jikar, which brushed across my shoulder and caught on the metal rings of my cuirass. That was his undoing.

I struck without mercy. By the time he finally stopped moving and his bowels let loose, blood had soaked both us and the snow and the sky above, it seemed.

I stumbled back to Halis, giddy with my triumph, and half-mad with the cold. The need to get back to civilization and wash the damned blood off my hands drove me. Her eyes opened wide at the sight of me. I laughed crazily, staring down at myself. How often had I spilled blood for these cursed Dela-Elan.

"Are you hurt?" she asked.

I shook my head. Then I realized that my ribs were piercing my insides and a strange red-tinged darkness was creeping up over my eyes. The world began spinning and my knees gave way. I landed hard on the ice.

The sun disappeared for a long time.

*

When I came to myself again it was late afternoon. The blood had dried on my shirt; I peeled it off and put on the one Halis had left draped around my shoulders.

[11]

Now, the pain of my wounds had lessened to equal that of my stomach.

Halis lay next to me in the snow, weak and tired, her eyes focused on some distant point.

"I heard their souls cry out as they were loosed from their bodies," she said softly. "They told me I will join them soon."

The sun cast cold, ever-lengthening shadows across the earth. Halis shivered from the slight wind.

"Stop such talk and get up, lady. We must find a place for the night."

Her eyes were sunken and ringed; her cheekbones protruded sharply from her face. "I couldn't move even if I wanted to."

"Your wound?"

She nodded weakly. I reached over to open her furs, but she clutched them together desperately. "I don't want you to see. It's putrefying."

A cold, merciless hand squeezed the beats from my heart. The life in my body seemed to drain into the snow beneath me.

She observed my expression. "I will go no further."

"Halis—"

"I will not!" she snapped, eyes flashing, jaw set.

I had been bodyguard to Halis for three years; I knew that expression and what it meant. She had made up her mind. She would not move and I was too weak from lack of food and my injuries to carry her the entire distance.

Her voice softened. "You must go on, Kem."

I shook my head. I, too, could be stubborn.

A look of desperate agony creased her face. "Go. I want you to live. I want someone to live on. Please." Tears shone in her eyes.

A strange twisting seized my stomach. I would not allow her pleas to affect me. I would not. No woman had affected me since . . .

My mother.

Why would I think of her now, though? She had no place inside me any longer.

I could no longer make sense of my feelings for Halis. It had been so much easier when I despised her for her status, her wealth, and her chain around my neck, no matter how silver and delicate.

After a long moment of silence she simply sighed and closed her eyes. She could not understand that I had no choice. She was Elan, the ruling elite; and more, Dela-Elan, elite of the elite. She had her place and I had mine. Here beside her, dying in the snow.

*

Hour after hour I sat in the snow next to her, watching the sun rise, the stars emerge, thinking of the sandy beaches and white cliffs of home. My life ran by in streams of memories. There were some memories I could not take. I folded up inside myself, expertly skirting the mirrored lake of deadness there, thick with the sludge of years.

I wondered if death was as the priests said: a darkened realm of ghosts and shades hovering about the living, forever grasping at food they could not taste and water they could not drink. Only brave soldiers and leaders of

[13]

state might be among the Honored Dead and live in the Night Palace.

Halis slept, pale face against paler snow, sighing every now and again, coughing more frequently. Once she woke, eyes unfocused and darker than I had ever seen them. I tried to give her water, but she brushed my hand away. Instead she sat halfway up, looking around her in confusion.

"Where is my blanket?"

"Right here," I said, tucking it around her chin.

"No," she said angrily, petulantly. "My purple blanket with the tassels. Mama always wraps it around me."

She was hallucinating, as I had seen so many near death do. Again I pulled the blanket over her.

"No! I want my blanket. Oh, where is it?"

And then she began crying like a tired child, fat tears rolling down her sunken cheeks, breath heaving and lips quivering.

I comforted her as best as I could, wiping the tears from her face and patting her back awkwardly. How thin and fragile she seemed. At last she slid into sleep again, lips parted and muscles relaxed in utter exhaustion.

For a long time I simply watched her: the darkness of her long curving eyelashes, the slightly parted lips, the sunken hollowness beneath her eyes. I reached out, intending to check the condition of her wound. Instead my hand drifted to a strand of her dark curly hair, rubbed it slowly between my fingers like fine silk.

Something shifted inside me so suddenly and powerfully that I could not help but stop and take notice: my carefully harbored deadness, breaking up like ice floes on the northern sea. Frightened, I scrabbled desperately to hold on to it. Halis was not like other people. She was Elan, the ruling elite: cruel, uncaring, oppressive. Keepers of slaves. Keepers . . . of the shrines; dark mysterious places where postulants knelt in the coolness, whispering their prayers to the gold-embossed marble statues. Canu and Korei, god and goddess of creation—balanced like sea and land, dark and light, male and female—

Female.

Like the sea. Deep and dark, powerful and cold, dangerous, but always harboring life within her.

Female.

Willful and obstinate, slim and dark, soft and desirable. Halis, hint of rosy-tipped breast, turn of a shoulder and wink of an eye. Laughter behind the beaded curtain, soft voice and softer moans of pleasure . . .

My mother, mad and dying.

Female.

When I realized at last what had been driving my life, the fear that had lurked like a specter behind every movement and decision, I began shuddering. I did not stop for a long time.

*

Time passed. I sat in the snow next to Halis, watching the pulse throb feebly at her throat, my limbs dragging with weakness and hunger and a lingering, numbing confusion worse than both of these.

I left only once, stumbling back to the Ulbari's bodies and stripping them of food: a handful of millet and two

[15]

small cakes of crumbly white cheese. I ate only a mouthful—enough to awaken my shrunken belly—before resuming my vigil at Halis's side.

Exhaustion assaulted me from within and unrelenting, oppressive whiteness from without. The world began coming and going in visions and dreams and scattered hallucinations until at last I found myself on a white sandy beach, just like home; warm sand, white-crested water, blue sky stretching into forever.

A movement caught my eye. I turned to see Halis walking barefooted along the surf toward me, her long, gauzy garments blowing in the wind. The brightness of the sun reflected off the white waves and white sand, making me seek refuge in her cool dark eyes. Her soft hair tousled across the strange, sad look on her face.

We stood facing each other, unspeaking. I had never wanted her more; the feeling gushed up through the deepest levels of my being, painful in its intensity. But my voice would not work and my legs would not move. A slight smile curved across Halis's lips.

"Go," she said softly. The glow around her grew brighter and hotter until I felt that it would burn me away into ashes—

I came to with a start. Silence swelled around me in waves like the stirring sea. Halis had walked the long road.

I stared at her quiet face and thought for a long moment about duty, how it had been my lifeblood for so long, and how I had never performed my duties for others, as I had thought, but for myself. Now there was only one duty left.

I gathered my belongings and stood on shaky knees, pausing long enough to scatter a few crumbs of food to

[16]

sustain her wandering spirit, before turning and walking away.

I headed toward the sea, which the people of Netria refer to as a woman; deep and dark, powerful and cold, dangerous at times, but always harboring life within her. It was time I joined them in that belief.

It was time I joined them in many things.

The Coming of the Destroyer

He came on a night pierced with stars and the shining moon, though an altogether unremarkable night except for its stillness.

I stood guard over my commander's grounds, a duty I had done many times before, and prided myself on. Relaxing at my post, I had no reason to worry, for the omen givers in the marketplace had promised an uneventful month, and I trusted their pronouncements. When the cry went up, then, it surprised me.

I ran to the main hall, my spear at the ready and my breastplate clanking. Fellow soldiers ran also, their sandaled feet slapping against the earth.

The prefect stood at the head of the well-lit hall, his body straight and tall, his head thrown back. His counselors flocked about him, but none of them dared to get close enough to touch. Ordinary men did not touch the prefect's robes. I thought, at first, that perhaps the prefect had fallen into a trance, but when he brought his head upright again I knew it was no such thing. His eyes shone bright with dismay, open so wide that the irises were ringed by white. I tensed with expectation.

"He has come tonight. The one we call the Great Outsider. The Alien. The Destroyer of our rule." The prefect's voice held no doubt.

As a soldier, a man of action, I did not shudder with fear. But many around me did.

"Go forth even now, my men. Go from city to city and capture this destroyer. Cease his advances. Bring me his head!" His voice echoed through the hall. "Look where he might be, and even where you are sure he might not be. Go one at a time, and know that if you fail we all do!"

Frightful words, powerfully spoken.

I proceeded from the hall, following my fellow soldiers. Once outside we parted in silence, each heading in a different direction across the darkened town. I went, padding softly. Fear scratched at my insides like a gnawing rodent.

The streets looked completely different at this hour, silent and naked of all human presence. Shadows danced, lamp lights flickered dimly, and night sounds replaced the bustle of the day. The tip of my spear glinted in the moonlight. A dog barked loud and close enough to startle me. I halted for a moment, catching my breath.

My mind spun with the knowledge that the fulfillment of the prophecy was here, at hand. The true origin of the prophecy supposedly lay in centuries past, but I had only heard it in the mouths of the court prophets in recent years. Still, it frightened me, for it told of a fearful warrior to come. A man who was both king and sun, whose advent heralded unthinkable disaster – the end of life as we knew it. Never had I faced a more important task. Stopping this abomination was bigger and more important than my own puny life.

Again I started jogging, searching the night for anything suspicious. After some time, I came to a hill outside of town. Something flashed out of the corner of my eye. I turned, seeking it out, and found that it was only a bright star. Then, a league or so on, a fork in the road and a choice. East or west?

East, something compelled me. The air brushed cool against my bare legs, and my tunic flapped against them as I moved.

I ran on, and I did not to grow weary. Casting my eyes to and fro, I searched for the Usurper, though I knew not where he would come from, nor what he would look like. Surely anything untoward would reveal him to me.

Time passed. I knew not how much. Neither did I care. Ahead, just over a gentle hill lay the outskirts of a small town. Two peasants walked quickly down the road toward me, whispering together in low, urgent tones.

"Halt!" I called.

Immediately, they did my bidding.

"Where do you go?"

They exchanged frightened glances, these two flat-faced peasants with dark eyes and thick curly hair, unremarkable in this desert land.

"Here now, what is your business?" I snapped.

The taller of the peasants hugged his trembling, robed body as if a cold wind blew from the west.

"We go on our master's bidding."

"Tell me."

The peasant searched my stern expression. He answered in a quavering voice, "To welcome he who our master wishes for us to welcome."

Connections fused and melted, as from lightning striking the metal statues atop the forum.

"The Destroyer!" I shouted.

The surprise and horror on their faces confirmed that I spoke the truth.

"Tell me where he is." My voice now came low and deadly.

"Please, do not make us betray our master!"

I threatened them with my spear. "Where is he?"

Wordlessly, they pointed back the way they had come, at a ramshackle type of hut barely visible through the dark. I rushed toward it, only seeing as I neared it that it was not a hut but instead a small feeding place for animals. What an odd dwelling place for the Destroyer! Perhaps, though, he was hiding. The glow of a torch leaked around mud brick walls, and low murmured voices came from within.

I stormed the building with a shout, skidding to a stop on scattered hay. A woman and a man looked up at me with terrified surprise. The woman held a baby in her arms. I said nothing for a moment, but only looked at them. Peasants both, their garments simple, their young faces twisted with worry. The child started to cry.

This was the end of life as we know it? The Toppler of Nations? The Great Enemy? A small baby boy.

I laughed in disgust, and jogged away.

The Pomegranate Tree

Iambe lay on her back on the stone table, looking up at Callithoe with wide dark eyes. Callithoe wet the sheet and wrung it as dry as she could.

"Must you do this, sister?" Iambe asked in a soft and rasping voice.

Callithoe glanced at her. "You know I must. Breathe slow and shallow, like we practiced."

As Callithoe neared her sister with the cloth, Iambe grasped her wrist. "What is the use? I will feed Cerberus at the River Styx one way or the other. It might as well be tonight."

Callithoe swallowed. Some statements did not deserve a reply, no matter how they twisted her innards.

Carefully, she spread the soaked sheet over Iambe's neck, then covered her face. Not like a burial shroud, she told herself. No, like a bandage instead – healing and protecting. The cloth molded around Iambe's lips, and rose and fell with her breath. Her precious breath.

Down here, they could not hear the fearful raging of the storm above, the way the winds whistled and murmured as they shook the palace above.

From leagues off, the storm had approached in a deep, dark purple mass that blotted out the sky from east to west, horizon to the heavens above. Moving relentlessly, it ate up the earth before it as a swarm of locusts devours green stalks of wheat.

Spotting it, the cold claw of fear seized Callithoe by the shoulders. The cursed dust storms came far too often since the drought began. Each time they visited, they stole away Iambe's vitality and put her back in her sick bed, coughing, wheezing, struggling to take breath after dirt-clogged breath.

Callithoe had snatched her sister's thin wrist and tugged her down dust-roughened stairs, around the corner of the storehouse and deep into the cistern below the palace, where water beaded on the walls and plopped in fat tinkling drops to the shallow pool at their feet. Here it was always cool, always quiet and safe from the dust that permeated everything else in the once-fragrant land.

Now, Callithoe breathed in the coolness, the humid clean air. In a low voice, she urged her sister, "Count the threads in Arachne's tapestry. Separate them in your mind, one by one, from the spindle. Notice the colors, and the textures. Think about what each one means. Think only of them."

She kept her hand resting lightly on Iambe's cloth-covered forehead until Iambe's breath settled into a slow rhythm.

Together, they waited.

*

By the time their middle sister Demo came to retrieve them, half the afternoon had passed. Callithoe's back and behind ached from perching beside Iambe on the stone table, soothing her with reminders to breathe

[23]

slow and steady, and encouraging her to keep heart. Demo assessed Callithoe in the dim torchlight.

"Go and rest," she said. "I will see to our sister."

Callithoe did not argue.

She did not rest, either. She headed for the well to soothe her parched throat.

Outside, dust lay over top of the withered world like newly fallen brown snow, fine and untouched. The Maiden Well lay only a few steps away. On the lip of the well, quiet and motionless, sat the robe-swathed figure of a woman.

Callithoe stopped in her tracks. Dust painted the woman from head to toe in a monotone brown. Only the slow blinking of her gaze distinguished her from a statue.

"Oh!" Callithoe exclaimed, when she found her voice.

She hurried to kneel like a child next to the woman. "Please, honored mother. Are you well?"

The olive tree that in former years had shaded the well and provided dark, delicious fruit for their table now held only one leafy branch, the rest spindly and dried. In the shade of that branch, Callithoe made out details she had not seen before: the woman's slumped shoulders, the tangles of wiry, gray-streaked hair, the dirt blackening her feet but leaving her slender ankles clean and white.

The woman observed her with strange pale eyes that reminded Callithoe of past years, of the great amber jewel her mother Metaneira had worn during the harvest festival.

Back when there was a harvest.

The woman looked at her, and unease struck Callithoe low in the belly. They seemed to be the eyes of some alien, unknowable creature, like a fearsome lion, or a hawk full-grown in its glory.

"Daughter?" she rasped.

Ah, thought Callithoe. So it was not something alien in her eyes, just something lost.

She put a hand gently on the woman's arm. "I am Callithoe, daughter of Celeus, king of Eleusis. You rest now at his well."

The woman gave a slight nod, her face seeming to awaken by degrees. Her eyes did not leave Callithoe's face.

"Young Callithoe, know you of a place where I might labor in exchange for a bed and meals? I have come so far, and escaped so much."

A rustle sounded beside Callithoe. Her third sister Cleisidice of the slender fingers knelt beside her. Callithoe had not even heard her approach.

"Pray tell us what you escaped, honored mother," beseeched Cleisidice.

Cleisidice. Always in the thick of things.

"Pirates who rode the wide back of the sea from Crete, where the bull-god reigns supreme. Then, after I escaped from them, I hid from slavers near the coast."

The sisters exchanged a glance. Lately, all manner of thieves and brigands had swept across the barren earth. Many had once been honest men. Want had made them lean and desperate.

"Worry not, dear mother," Cleisidice said. "You are far from such villains here at Eleusis."

She drew a cup of water from the well and handed it to the woman. Particles of dust sprinkled the water like some sort of fine seasoning. She drank.

"Come," Callithoe said, decisive in her role as eldest daughter. She stood and offered the woman her arm. "Share of our table, and sleep safe from your trials."

The woman complied, rising to stand taller than both sisters. The scent of many long miles clung to her, and dust caked the lines about her mouth.

"Doso," she said. "You may call me Doso."

Cleisidice offered her a tentative smile, then extended her arm. Doso accepted it.

"Pirates, you say?" Cleisidice asked with shameless curiosity. "We must know. However did you escape them?"

*

Doso stayed.

In the end, it was as simple as that. Oh, Callithoe knew the story had more twists and turns than that: whispered conversations, sly tests, and even pleading tears, on Cleisidice's part. Cleisidice, who had formed an immediate attachment to the unfortunate woman. Doso, she had discovered, had escaped the pirates by hiding by the stern-cables when the boat had been put ashore for the evening.

The more pressing reason for Doso's place here, however, had to do with Metaneira's need to care for both Iambe and Demophon. Demophon, a five year old menace of endless energy and mischief.

"You are blessed among mortals, young Demophon," said Doso, when first she met him, out in the garden. The workmen barely kept it alive by toting water in jugs from the thin trickle of a river beyond.

Doso's pronouncement caused Demophon to stop in the midst of dashing after an arthritic old hunting dog that had once accompanied Celeus across the marshes. He looked up at Doso, all brown inquisitive eyes and chubby cheeks, his hair a wild riot of curls.

"What's a mortal?" he asked.

Doso, scrubbed clean and wearing a blue peplos that mother had given her, smiled at him. "A mortal is something that lives and breathes and rejoices in all that this flawed and wondrous world has to offer."

"'Joices?" he asked skeptically. "I don't 'joice."

For indeed, Demophon always let it be known that he disagreed with whatever one was telling him at the time.

Doso bent near, as though to whisper a secret. Demophon inclined his head to listen. Instead, Doso wrinkled up her nose and, making pincers of her fingers, seized Demophon by the middle and tickled him until he howled with laughter.

"Not 'joicing," he protested. "Not 'joicing!"

But he could not resist the tickles, and Doso could not resist smiling.

The expression looked so unusual on her. Sorrow had seemed etched in the delicate skin around her eyes.

"You are rejoicing even now, little man!" she teased.

Demophon shrieked and dashed around a statue of Apollo, one eye over his shoulder in a clear invitation for Doso to chase him.

The smile still on her lips, Doso lumbered after him like a great old mother bear.

*

Callithoe gauged the hours that passed by the length of the shadows that fell upon the furniture in the room she and Iambe shared, and by the changing color of the light – nearly white to yellow to burnt orange. She treasured the hours, and if she could have snatched them from the air like bees or grasshoppers, she would have put them in a woven basket as keepsakes. She hated to think of the future, and what it might bring.

Instead, she pulled a chair close to Iambe's couch, close enough that she might put a hand on her arm. She did her best to distract her sister with stories of the gods, the demigods, and those favored humans who had been visited by them. It seemed to keep her mind off the coughing.

Callithoe knew many stories. She of all in her household remembered the best details from the minstrels who recited their tales at the festivals. Her favorites were the comedies. She treasured the fleeting smiles upon Iambe's lips.

At the end of one such tale, Iambe declared in a low wheeze, "The gods are cruel."

Callithoe's chest squeezed. She swallowed. "I know it must seem so. Perhaps, because of this, we should favor the goddesses instead."

Iambe's breath sounded like the laboring pumps of the blacksmith's bellows.

"Oh, Callithoe. You are always telling me falsehoods to lift my spirits. They are not working today."

"You are wrong! All stories have a certain kind of truth in them. The best kind, for they explain to us why things are the way they are."

Iambe's eyes welled with angry tears. "Then explain it to me. Why am I sick? What evil have I committed?"

"Sister, you have committed no such evil. You know that."

"Then it is merely the whims of the gods, that I am sick and that you and our other siblings are not."

"Iambe—"

"See? There is no excuse, save that the gods are cruel."

Callithoe put her hand on Iambe's moist cheek. "How can they be, little sister?" She smiled, quiet and small, and put all the force of her devotion into her words, "They gave you to me."

*

Iambe slept at last, thinly and miserably. Callithoe left their room silently, creeping like a cat. She went to the kitchen with some notion of helping with dinner.

Doso, alone there, put olives in the press to extract oil. She glanced at Callithoe, frowning. "You do her no favors. Empty promises, that's all you offer her. She has sensed the way of things, the truth, but you will not allow her to keep it."

"What? Are you talking about Iambe?"

Doso grimaced, exasperated. "Of course, Iambe. I know that she weeps at the cruelty of the gods."

Emotion rose up in Callithoe. "How can you know such a thing? Have you spied on us?"

Doso gave a harsh laugh. "I have no need to spy. I smell the loathsome piety all over you, the scent of the laurel tree."

"How dare you speak to me with such disrespect!"

Doso shoved aside the press with sudden violence, and approached like a mad thing, like a wild woman. Callithoe shrank back. Doso's words flew like poisoned arrows.

"Is it disrespect to speak of truth to one who believes lies? You do not know what I know, maiden. You do not know how young life can be snatched in a cruel instant. How even though you sheltered her and nourished her, and carefully planned for her life – her blessed life – the gods might despise your feeble efforts." Doso's voice resonated through the room, past the close walls, like the shrieking of a bird in distress – high and relentless.

Spittle flew from her lips. Her eyes blazed. "Oh, no. You don't know how they turn on everyone – even on their own, and they snatch away that sweet young thing, that beautiful, innocent daughter. They call it a slip, an accident. 'She hit her head on the rocks, mother. It is no one's fault.' But you know the truth, that the King of Hell took her – he who rides a chariot pulled by dark frothing steeds. He dragged her down into the underworld. She tried to come back to you – she would always try to come back – but he wouldn't let her."

She paused, eyes travelling far away, as though she had just heard the words she had spoken. Tears erupted, then. "I looked for her. I flew from place to place, crying after her ..." Her voice petered out, transforming into sobs. Bitter, lonely sobs. They sounded like flesh tearing, like the wailing of the damned on the sea of fire. Doso keened, pulling at her hair, her face twisted.

Movement attracted Callithoe's attention. Metaneira and Cleisidice, both of them dark-haired and solemn-faced, stood in the doorway. Of course they had heard. Of course everyone had heard.

Little footsteps ran up. Demophon, wide-eyed and solemn. He took in the scene without fear. To his child's mind tears were no strange thing.

"Nurse!" he cried. "Don't cry, dear nurse."

He went to her, and put his hand on her arm, heedless of her red face and the grief so explosive that she shook with it. He buried his face in her breast, hushing her like she had hushed him so many times.

"Dear nurse," he repeated. "Dear, dear nurse."

The torrent of tears increased for a few moments as she clung to him, her gnarled hand gentle as she stroked his hair.

"You are feeding the rivers, nurse," he told her, after a moment.

She gave a little laugh, sniffling. Callithoe recognized the words as ones Doso herself had used when Demophon wailed about something so devastating and trite that he forgot about it in the next moment, as children do so often.

Callithoe felt the approach of her mother and sister behind her. The three of them withdrew as of one mind, letting Doso gather what comfort she could in the arms of the youngest among them.

They waited by the bronze door of the temple, Callithoe and the priestesses, and King Celeus's guards in their cuirasses and lances, their helmets shining smartly.

"It will be bad today," warned the head priestess. The lines on her face had deepened into chasms these past years. Though she had grown gaunt and stooped, her voice still rang with authority.

"Stand back when I command it," directed Menos, the head guard. He nodded at the four other guards. Callithoe saw only their eyes, brown and anxious, and their lips, resolved and thin, around the crossbars of their helmets. "Do not allow tenderness to cloud your minds. They are ravening beasts at times such as these."

Then Menos opened the door and the harsh afternoon sun burst across the cool darkness of the temple storehouse. The noise of the poor waiting there rose like a great wind upon the sea. Callithoe flew into action, scooping the grain from the storage vessels.

"Here, here!" cried the voices.

Outstretched bowls and open sacks and humble woven baskets thrust toward her, one on top of another. The poor lunged, desperate and wild-eyed. Old and young, male and female, they became alike in their hunger and want.

"Fall back!" Menos ordered. "Be patient! You will each get a turn."

Callithoe emptied her bowl into a near sack, spilling a little in her haste. The owner of the sack pulled it open again. "More! Please, my child weeps for bread!"

Callithoe ignored that plea, and the others, busying herself with the physical motions of scooping the grain, emptying it, pushing away the filled vessels.

The scene repeated itself every month on the new moon. The poor clamored at the door in their threadbare clothing. The grain from the king's warehouses had grown less as the years of the famine multiplied into seven, now. Wise Celeus himself allocated the rations. Deep in the storehouses the reserve from the years of plenty had become so depleted that it would run out entirely soon.

Once, whole herds of lambs and goats had swarmed over the hills. How those hills had echoed with the bells on their collars, the bleating calls of the young. So many had been killed for food or died off from disease, made weak by the lack of forage that few remained. Likewise the poor had died off, the babes in arms, the little children and the old and feeble. Callithoe had visited the makeshift hospitals and nursed them as she could. After a while she had stopped coming, though. She could not dwell so much on their great suffering, their miserable plight. She could not bear it.

She concentrated on counting the bowls of grain she distributed. At twenty-three only dregs remained from the storage vessels. Scooping up the remains with her bare hands, she let them fall into the bowl of a thin boy with a festering sore on his lip.

"Please, we need more!" he beseeched her. "My mother is ill! I cannot go home with this – it will barely last us the week."

"I'm sorry—"

Menos thrust his lance between them, pushing the child away. The boy's eyes widened as a look of stark agony transformed his face. He began to shriek, high and unintelligible, as though a snake bit him or a slave master beat him. His red face, tear-stained face disappeared as the guards cursed and shoved back the others who filled the gap the boy had made.

Callithoe stumbled back as the guards protected her and the priestesses from the rabble. With deep shouts and brutal efficiency, they ejected the remaining poor from the temple and barred the doors.

She stood there panting with the other women. They looked at one another, silent. No one needed to say it. The feeding of the poor had never been an easy task, but this time it was worse than ever.

*

Callithoe marched alongside her father's guards as evening fell. Her sandals kicked up little puffs of dust on the dry, beaten-down path to the palace. No one spoke. The faces of the many poor, the look of panic and desperation on the boy's face ... she could not seem to clear her mind of the images.

To the west, Apollo drove his chariot the sun over the edge of the earth in a brilliant splash of orange and fiery red. Streaks of clouds, glowing and otherworldly, spread across the sky smears of paint, melancholy and beautiful.

A great, unbearable sadness came over her. The burden was so sudden and so heavy that she stopped in her tracks. An abandoned manger, with tumbled walls and spindly weeds growing up all about it, faced the path.

"Lady?" asked Menos, resonant and wary.

"Go on," she directed. "I wish to stay here alone."

Menos frowned. "Your father will not approve."

[34]

"My father cares only for my wellbeing." She gestured around at the empty place. "I am safe here, Menos. Can you not see? Go on."

He considered her statement. Past behavior told her that he would not hesitate to ignore her wishes entirely, if it meant her safety. But the poor had long vanished into their hovels. She had lingered at the temple to make sure they would not meet any on the way home.

He nodded, still looking warily at her. What had he heard in her voice? She suppressed the urge to give a bitter laugh.

With a few muttered commands the guards turned and marched away in a little, regimented knot. The bronze of their spear tips prodded the darkening sky; their helmeted heads looked forward only, not to the side or back. Always forward, single-minded and resolute.

She sagged to a broken wall, her eyes on the sunset, ever changing and brilliant, transforming and dying moment by moment. Fixing her mind on the memory of Mother Rhea's statue, she pictured how it stood clothed in a peplos of finest dyed purple linen paused in mid-motion, arm lifted to hail some invisible person, knee pressed against the roaring lion that traveled alongside her. She had often been the one to weave the statue's fresh laurel wreath herself, to place it on Mother Rhea's head. Afterward that whole day at odd intervals she smelled the laurel scent on her fingers.

Her eyes burned as she began to pray. "Oh, Mother. Dear Mother ..."

With all her strength, she prayed for Iambe, for the poor, for the land suffering so long in drought. Oh, how bitter it was to pray for the parched and cracked land, where even thistles and weeds struggled to grow, for the prayers brought to mind better times, greener fields and the scent of blossoms. Doso's name came to her lips as well, that her heart might be softened toward the gods, toward all good things despite the burdens of daily sorrow she suffered under.

She did not know how long she sat there, her thoughts focused on the goddess. Long enough for the sunset to dull and darken. The noise of buzzing night insects brought her out of her fervent prayers. She blinked. The bowl of the dark gray sky above her would soon be obsidian black. She stood. The stiffness of her backside revealed that she had slumped atop the broken wall for longer than she intended.

It scarcely mattered, though. She knew her way home, which lay just down this hill and over one other. Hurrying, she looked down in an effort avoid the stones in the path. Rustles in the brush startled her; a flock of night doves burst from the skeleton of a bush, squawking and protesting. Her breath sped, and sweat dampened her hairline and underarms. When she topped that second hill and saw a lamp flickering in the window of the palace, she sighed in relief.

A branch cracked not a stadium from her. She could see nothing in the gloom. Then, a low growl – a sinister reverberating scream far too loud to come from a small, inoffensive creature. Rather, it must be something lanky and large. With sharp incisors and a hungry belly. Something that could be waiting to ambush her if she didn't hurry.

Heart pounding, she ran. She fixed her eyes on the palace and abandoned her careful pace, running as fast as she dared.

Brush broke behind her. Pure terror jolted her. Another growl sounded. This one closer, and louder. Panic bit like the whip-crack strike of a viper. She forced herself to keep her wits about her, though it would have been far too easy to give into gibbering terror. Instead she focused on the palace walls ahead and on the motion of her legs, which seemed far too slow. She would get home. She would!

Though she expected to feel the crunch of teeth on bone and sinew, it never came. She made it to the front of the palace, flew up the front steps, and threw herself through the door.

She flattened herself against the wall, her mind thundering: Safe! Safe! I am safe at last!

Metaneira and her sisters gathered around her, asking, "What chases you, Callithoe?"

Demo and Cleisidice stroked her face and shoulders, murmuring soothing words. Her father the king called the guards that they might search the night for the wild beast.

*

The guards found nothing. Such did not surprise her, given the darkness of the night, devoid even of the moon.

"It was probably a wolf, separated from its pack," said Menos, in an attempt to calm Callithoe.

"It was not a wolf," she replied testily. "It was too big. No wolf makes sounds like that."

Menos looked at Metaneira and Celeus with barely veiled exasperation. "Perhaps. We have done all that we can for the night. We will search for it at first light."

"Of course," said the king.

He went to Callithoe, and laid his heavy, ringed hand on the crown of her head, like he used to when she was a child. "Sleep, daughter. The gods have blessed us with your safe return tonight."

The excitement of the evening had ebbed at last, and indeed Callithoe's eyes burned with fatigue. Iambe, weak still from her latest bout with illness, had retired to their chambers a while ago. Callithoe followed her, thinking that her exhaustion would result in a long, deep sleep.

She could not have been more mistaken. She lay awake, tormented by the echoes of the beast's screams, replaying the wild flight toward home, and before that, the desperate scrambles of the poor for food. At last, she discarded her stubborn attempts to sleep and rose. Iambe slept on, making that soft snoring noise that she always denied when Callithoe teased her about it in the light of day.

Pausing outside her door, she heard a murmur, followed by the fretful protest of a child, cut short. Demophon. She padded down the cool stone hallway in her bare feet. How odd that he would be awake so late, when all the palace lay sleeping. Perhaps his nightmares had returned.

Wind blew in a low, fitful moan, causing the shutters to snap against the window frame. Standing shock still and listening, she at length decided that it lacked the strength to become another awful dust storm. The fearful twisting of her gut abated.

Another murmur came. Doso's voice, from the hearth room.

Callithoe saw the yellow glow of the hearth before she entered the room. How strange that Doso had built a fire so high. The heat of the summer days kept them from building the fire during the night.

She stepped into the room.

Doso stood before the hearth, illuminated by the tall bright flames. Her peplos was unbelted and her hair a frizzy tree canopy with strands knotted and pointed outward like branches. She held a large animal or weighted sack from her thin wrist – something that Callithoe could not identify – over the flames. Doso shifted at Callithoe's appearance, as did the angle of her strange burden. Callithoe beheld human eyes, glassy and dazed.

Demophon!

Directly over the flames he dangled from his heel. He hung slack and light, as if he weighed no more than a dried husk of wheat or a handful of feathers.

"Stop!" Callithoe heard herself shriek.

She rushed at the bizarre sight, hands outstretched like claws. Crazed with fear for her brother, she snatched at Doso's peplos with one hand and used it as leverage to grab at Demophon with the other.

A great blow struck her in the midsection. She flew backward like a bird in a sudden updraft. Striking her head against a marble support column, she crumpled to the floor. Her ears rang and pain blazed across the back of her head. She forced her senses back in order.

"Demophon!" she called.

Callithoe got to her knees. The world pitched and heaved around her like the deck of a storm-ravaged ship.

Doso's face twisted with loathing. "I'm saving him, stupid girl! The elemental fire will make him immortal."

Mother Rhea, no!

Callithoe struggled to stand, but her eyes refused to stay focused. Behind her, she heard the cries of her sisters and mother erupting in dismay.

"Guards! Attend us at once!" Celeus shouted. He had appeared from somewhere, sword in hand.

He lunged at Doso, exclaiming, "Back, foul creature!"

Motion, beside her. A harsh laugh from Doso and Celeus's sword flew through the room like a twig carried by a mighty wind. The king collided with the hearth grate and stumbled, his leg bent in an awkward, unnatural angle.

The wooden shutter banged open. Wind howled through the open window and whirled into a tornado. It doused the yellow flames with a great whoosh. Sand and grit pelted them with stinging needles. A great cloud of ash from the hearth billowed outward, momentarily obscuring Doso.

"Mother Rhea," cried Metaneira. "Have mercy on us!"

When the smoke cleared, Doso stood facing them with an expression of cold disdain. "Take him, then! You puling ingrates are not worthy of such an honor."

She swung Demophon like a stone in a sling. He tumbled across the stone floor limply, arms and legs sprawling. Metaneira leapt for him. Gathering him up, she cradled him in her arms with a choked cry. He stirred, whining with confusion.

A terrible animal shriek rent the air. Weak flames had revived enough to illuminate the room. A form blurred past them as big as a man but four-legged and hip-height. Callithoe glimpsed thick paws and tan, lanky shoulders. A mountain lion! The very same creature, she knew with sudden inspiration, that she had encountered hours earlier.

The lion leapt, two front paws hitting Doso in the chest and bringing her down to the tiles. It screamed in conquest, white teeth gleaming. The two rolled about in a desperate struggle for dominance. Doso used her fragile human nails like claws, grunting and shrieking like an animal herself.

Arms closed around Callithoe's shoulders and pulled her back. Her father the king, tugging her away. Dragging and sweating, they headed for Iambe and her other sisters. Metaneira pulled Demophon with her as she shrank away to the far wall.

Thunder cracked, close and startlingly loud.

Doso grabbed at a fire poker with a scrabbling hand. Twisting, she swung at the lion. A huge paw swiped the iron aside easily. Darting down, teeth bared, it went for Doso's throat. Simultaneously, the lion used its front legs like arms, wrapping them around her body. Planting its hind legs, it dragged her backward, jaws locked on the back of her throat.

Doso flailed helplessly. "No! He let Hades kill my sweet Persephone. I will never return to him!"

The mountain lion rumbled deep and loud. As if in answer.

"Help me, King Celeus!" Doso implored.

"Oh!" Metaneira cried, hands at her mouth. She held Demophon to her breast.

The lion tugged Doso toward the open window. A flash of lightning exploded at the same instant that a tremendous boom of thunder sounded. The palace shook with reverberations.

The brilliant white lightning illuminated the lion's eyes. The afterimage of those eyes seared into Callithoe's mind as the brightness blinded her. Eyes that were green and intelligent. Like the eyes of a human.

A terrible shriek came from Doso. It sounded like death, like the very voice of pain. By the time Callithoe's eyes cleared the room was empty.

Metaneira stood clutching Demophon still. "We are saved! Thanks be to Mother Rhea!"

Callithoe gave a half-hysterical giggle. Her head throbbed and she felt dizzy and dazed with sudden relief. "Do not forget Zeus. The Loud Thunderer speaks even yet."

Callithoe clung to her sisters, all of them breathing hard, sniffling, and dabbing at tears.

Demophon came back to himself, querulous, seeming not to know what had happened to him, and not any worse for it.

By the time they nailed the shutter back together, rain had begun to pour from the heavens.

*

The guards went out to search for Doso and the lion at the break of day, but the heavy rain, thunder and lightning hampered their efforts. Menos tracked paw prints in the ground for a stadium before they seemed to vanish into thin air. The guards ranged afield, looking for shreds of Doso's peplos, bloody clumps of her hair, or perhaps torn remnants of her body.

That evening, Callithoe watched as Menos came to report his findings to King Celeus. His long face looked even more somber than usual.

"Nothing," he said. "We searched to the temple and back again. It is as if Zeus himself carried them away to Olympus."

King Celeus looked at her, troubled. Once he might have punished the guards for their failure. Now, he said nothing.

The rain continued for three days straight.

Doso's story made the rounds like a rabid animal. The priestesses in the temple disdained the wet and the wind and visited the palace's hearth room as though it were a place of holy delight. Soon the elders of the town took up that same pilgrimage, followed afterward by a seemingly endless train of onlookers.

The fury of the rain lessened until it sprinkled the terra cotta vessels with gentle pings, allowing Metaneira to prop open the doors. A cool, fresh smelling breeze chased the stale grit from the palace's inner rooms. It even swept away the scent of sickness that hung in heavy curtains around Iambe's couch.

The tailings of such breezes brought snatches of conversation and gossip to Callithoe's ears.

"... her eyes glowed red ... flames shot from her fingers ... Demeter was her name ... "

How strange that Doso's plain and simple name now became that of Demeter. Demeter, of all things! Remote and fertile, a wooden, lifeless hearth goddess made suddenly real. Callithoe might have corrected their error, if it she thought it would do any good. The people knew that something strange and marvelous had happened, something which they did not altogether understand.

On the fourth day, bright and early, the sun rose as if in triumph, its light making jewels of the water droplets that lay over the whole earth.

Iambe rose from her couch, her cheeks glowing pink and her eyes alight. Her breath came easy. She took Callithoe's hand, twining their fingers together.

Together, they walked out the palace's front doors. Callithoe's sandals squished and slid on the mud. The entire household followed them, blinking in the bright light, murmuring in pleasure. Women stood in little knots, children playing about their feet. Men also walked the pathways in twos and threes, canvassing fields that had been barren for so many months.

Callithoe and Iambe paused at the Maiden Well, under the shade of the old olive tree. Doso had first appeared there, on the low marble wall.

"Look," Iambe said. Tears shown at the corner of her eyes.

She held out her hand. The crisp olive leaves shone with drying rain. In the midst of the tiny bouquet they formed lay the new growth of a small brown fruit.

[44]

Part II

Where fantasy meets anthropology

The stories of Janet Loftis

Skin Job

In his hand was death...and life. Death to the viricamas, the witches...to Uida should he find her. May the goddesses have mercy on him, forgive him his shame, grant him his revenge.

Bellar rubbed his thumb over the pure, lethal crystals, careful to not spill the precious supply — precious because of his stupidity. They seemed so fragile, so starkly white against the dark skin of his palm. They would be his salvation.

As the half moon rose over the far edge of the ravine, Bellar held out his handful of salt so the light could bathe the crystals. They sparkled like fireflies or like Uida's eyes when she rode him—

"Fool!" Esaf barked. "You wish to drop all we have left in the witches' own pit!"

Bellar did not flinch. Esaf had never been the quietest of hunters; Bellar had heard him approach and, knowing Esaf's gruff demeanor, had expected such an outburst. They were friends.

"I wanted Kaja," the moon goddess, "to bless our weapon." He carefully slid the salt back into the pouch hanging from his belt.

He turned to look at Esaf as he asked, "Have you found a way down?"

Esaf nodded just as a cloud obscured the moon, putting them into darkness. Bellar had a moment to consider that, being Esaf's skin was the darkest of all their tribesmen, in the totality of night he could not be seen at all. Perfect for hunting their quarry — if only he could be silent.

And totality of night was where they were going: down into the ravine itself. Into the vira, as the wise women had named it, into what should never be seen by mortal eyes.

With Esaf leading the way, they skirted the edge of the ravine until they reached a narrow cleft which looked like it had been carved out by an ancient waterfall.

"It's steep, but passable," Esaf said as he swung his legs over the edge. He looked up at the moon. "Say goodbye to Kaja."

For we may not see her again, Bellar finished the thought himself, then shook his head at his own pessimism. He would kill Uida. He would.

As they half-slid, half-climbed down toward the darkened tangle of treetops below Bellar kept an eye on the sky above. Not just for a last glimpse of Kaja's blessed light, but for—

There. One ball of fire, like a mass of angry red fireflies, rose from the canopy. It brilliantly lit up the trees below it, like a torch moving over the forest as the fireball soared in the direction of their village.

The two men flattened themselves against the walls of the cleft as the fireball passed nearly overhead. Then they waited, feet slipping on the loose soil, hands clutching jagged edges of rock. After what seemed an interminable amount of time, a second fireball emerged from the canopy and passed over just to the south.

"So...now we find out if Kenar was right," Esaf muttered. "Are there just two remaining like he said, or three?"

Bellar prayed for two. They waited, until Bellar's arms began to cramp from the strain of holding himself in place. "Two," he pronounced, hopefully with conviction.

Esaf did not move, except for his eyes which scanned the trees. Bellar knew his hunting partner had committed to memory the locations from where the fireballs originated, and was now waiting for a third. That kind of concentration was why Bellar had asked him to come along. And because he was his friend. When others — what few other men were left — had volunteered to come along, Bellar said no. It was his right to decide on the hunting party members; he was after all the Codro Sal, or salt-keeper, the guardian of the brine wells. So the others had not questioned him, even though his true motivation for bringing Esaf was that if Bellar's shame was to be revealed by the viricamas, he could bear no one but a friend knowing.

Finally, Esaf took his eyes off the trees, and began the descent again.

By the time they reached the bottom both men were scraped and dirtied, but neither paid it heed. They had until just before sunrise to find their quarry in this forest, which wasn't a long time at the height of summer.

Still, Esaf paused before entering the dark, brooding, vine-covered trees. "Remember the stories?" he asked softly.

"My sister—" Bellar choked off a rush of emotion, "used to think it was funny to terrify me with demon

[49]

stories. It kept me awake at night so I'd be too tired to do my chores the next day and then my father would punish me for being lazy."

Esaf looked at him, sadness plain in his eyes. "I am sorry."

"How was she to know the stories were true?" He tried to make it sound lighthearted, but knew he failed miserably. How could Nedisse have known her husband would be ravaged by a viricama, and that her own immense love for him would drive her to intervene, so that it was she whose life was taken instead. Now Benno, her husband, wasted away in his own grief, a burnt shell of a man and a burden to the tribe.

They were not stories; they were not women. Witches and other evil spirits inhabited the vira. Before the current crisis no one but fools had dared to enter the vira in more than two generations — none of them had ever returned. Nor did any of the brave hunters before Esaf and Bellar return even though they had succeeded in reducing the number of viricamas to two. At this moment, Bellar's and Esaf's remaining families were preparing their mourning rituals, and then, abandoning the village. If the two men were not back by midday, they would be presumed dead and left behind. By the following morning, the Nabil Eade would no longer exist as a tribe because their home formed part of their identity. The tribe would journey beyond the mountains bordering their homeland and take a new name. And Bellar and Esaf would be forgotten — on purpose.

Neither man dwelled on what could be their fate, but both knew their actions were necessary. The attacks by the viricamas had risen in frequency and were no longer restricted to the men; women now died equally, especially the pregnant ones. The wise women believed that was how the viricamas had grown in number so rapidly as of late; it was said that the fetuses of the dead mothers-to-be were no longer with the bodies, that they were taken and...changed...made into women that were not women.

Uida....

The one thing they did not expect in the vira was silence; silence that allowed Bellar's questions and doubts to echo in his mind. The stories were filled with sound: especially the agonized shrieking of the viricama's victims as their disembodied souls relived the memory of their flesh burning or cried for revenge they could never have. Nedisse's stories had always included an animal of some sort, a companion demon whose unearthly howls she reenacted with such spine-tingling enthusiasm that Bellar — as a young boy — would wet himself.

In the real vira there was none of that.

"Do—" Esaf stopped as his voice unexpectedly boomed rather than being muffled by the dense foliage. Whispering, he continued, "do you suppose they've killed all the animals here?"

Bellar nodded thoughtfully. "They truly are consumers of life — all life..." He fingered a thick, broad leaf, "...except this."

"They need meat," Esaf said roughly.

"Or something with a soul," Bellar concluded, but only to himself as Esaf was already pushing forward again homing in ever closer to the location fixed in his mind.

The heat grew oppressive as they plunged deeper into the vira. Soon, Bellar's skin felt like it was on fire. He knew it was just sweat popping from his pores, but it did not feel like the sweat from chopping wood for the fires to boil the brine or like the sweat generated by the heat of those fires. Bellar reached up and rubbed his fingers across his cheek, stuck them in his mouth. Too salty, as if the salt were purposefully being drawn from his body.

The gesture reminded Bellar too much of the moment when he realized Uida was a witch. Her taste — it had been all wrong. A woman's juices were salty just like a man's (so he'd been told), but in that momentarily delightful instant after he'd had his hand inside her and then, in anticipation, had raised his fingers to his mouth wanting to lick them, wanting to savor that womanly taste.... His stomach churned.

Esaf hissed. "You lose yourself too much in your mind, Codro Sal." His eyes, all of him that Bellar could see, were accusatory. Then, taking Bellar's chin in his hand, turned Bellar's face so that he was looking into a tiny clearing.

At first, Bellar saw nothing, but as his eyes slowly focused upon the unmoving grass...there...a pale pile of skin. Their quarry.

"Go," Esaf said, releasing Bellar's chin. "I'll find the other." He squeezed between two tree trunks and disappeared back into the forest.

Was Esaf afraid to enter the clearing? Bellar pondered that for a moment knowing it was more an excuse to delay action than a question he needed answered. After another moment's hesitation, he stepped forward with one hand clutching his salt pouch. Murmuring the traditional salt blessing he took one careful step after another until he stood looking down at it. He would not label it a her.

Bellar crouched for a long moment before he could bring himself to touch it. He wouldn't need to touch it at all if not for his own stupidity; he could simply sprinkle the salt and be done with it if he didn't need to know whether or not it was Uida. But the skin was loosely folded, lumped on itself, hiding the face.

He didn't know what he expected. It didn't quite feel like skin, but he couldn't describe it as rubbery or like animal hide or fur or feathers...maybe more like softened bone. And it was warm. He had imagined it would be cold, but then Uida had been so hot.

Steeling himself for disappointment or satisfaction, he flipped the face over. Surprise. It was not Uida, but then he would never have suspected that Magala was a viricama. But there was no mistaking the mottled birthmarks covering Magala's face. Or her ragged hair and the way it hung down over her eyes. Those empty pockets seemed to stare at him just as her eyes would during the moon rituals. Now they mocked him: Magala was a priestess of Kaja. Did that corrupt all he knew of Kaja? Did the goddess who claimed to protect his village really seek to destroy it?

For a very long moment Bellar stared at those empty eye pockets, not knowing what to do or to believe. Too many questions reeled in his mind.

Only a chirping whistle, repeated three times, broke him out of his disturbance. Esaf. He'd found the other skin.

Quickly, Bellar emptied half of the salt into his palm and began carefully sprinkling the white death on

Magala's skin. Salt, the only true protection against evil spirits, the only true barrier, would prevent the viricama from reentering its skin; when the sun arose while the viricama was still in its fiery form, fire would kill fire. The witch would die.

He hesitated only once as he did this, wondering if his offering the salt to Kaja for blessing would have the reverse effect. The whistling came again — impatient this time. Finished, Bellar secured the pouch and ran in the direction from which Esaf called.

Another tiny clearing, another pile of skin.

Esaf again held back from entering the clearing as Bellar, confident this time that his revenge was at hand, began sprinkling the rest of the salt on Uida. Wanting, purely for perverse reasons, to rub the salt around her empty mouth as if he could erase the memory of her lips pleasuring him, he turned the face toward him—

Who was this? He didn't recognize this witch at all. Could it be one of the prematurely-aged stolen fetuses?

"What is it?" Esaf called softly.

Bellar looked over his shoulder. "Kenar was wrong. There are three left."

"How do you know?"

He almost couldn't bring himself to say it, not even to his friend. "It's not Uida."

Esaf closed his eyes, effectively disappearing from Bellar's sight. His voice seemed to come from no where. "She cannot be...."

Bellar didn't understand Esaf's strange tone.

[54]

"She is." Bellar put what was left of the salt back into his pouch while hoping it would be enough for one last skin. "There is no salt in her. None that I could taste." Esaf would know what that meant. They often talked about their women; Bellar could not explain why he'd kept his liaison with Uida a secret.

Esaf's eyes flew open. "If she is viricama, then what are you?"

Bellar paused halfway between Esaf and the salted skin. He didn't know what to say.

Esaf seemed to forget his fear of the clearing and began advancing upon him. "All the other men who'd been sexed by a viricama are either burned or dead. How did you survive?"

He tried to lie. "It wasn't—"

"You sexed her. I saw." Esaf paused for only the briefest of moments and began speaking hurriedly, "The others were concerned about you, about the Codro Sal being alone and vulnerable to attack while tending to the brine wells so I was assigned to protect you, to follow you." Following him secretly went without saying: the brine wells were considered so vital to the tribe's existence that no one but the Codro Sal could know their location; it was a secret passed from father to son for generations. Not even Esaf, one of the potters who supplied the pots for the boiling of the brine, knew.

"I saw much: how strangely you behaved after sexing her, how strange it was for you not to share her," as they'd done with other women — an acceptable practice among the unmarried men of their tribe, "...but I said nothing...nothing...." Esaf trailed off, clearly distressed.

"It was only sex." Like none other. He had yearned for it every moment he was away from her, could hardly think of anything but the heat of her mouth around him.

"But I never told Kenar or the others what I saw."

Those words seemed to have such import, Bellar questioned them, "What else did you see?"

"I saw you destroy the brine wells."

Bellar stood still in shock. It was several moments before he could find his voice. "I did not."

"You did."

"No." That was not his shame. "Uida tricked me into revealing the wells' location." He remembered clearly telling Uida how to find them, how he'd felt helpless to resist her questions.

"I saw you."

"No, it was Uida." Wasn't it? He remembered little of the night before except how Uida had finally, after so many nights of sexing, presented herself as a meal. She knew how he loved tasting women; he'd begged for her juices in his mouth. It'd been like she was giving him a gift. But could the gift have been meant for the viricamas instead? Perhaps she had bewitched him. He didn't know what to think, but knew his silence now was only serving to make Esaf more certain of his own beliefs.

Bellar closed the distance between them. "But you owe more to the tribe than to me, even as my friend. Why would you remain silent if what you saw was true?"

"I thought...maybe...you were trying to save us. To convince the tribe to move away from here before we sacrificed all our men to the viricamas. I thought you were desperate after losing Nedisse and overburdened by caring for her crippled husband."

Esaf was silent for a moment. "Then you volunteered for this mission and I didn't know what to think. Were you trying to make up for a terrible deed, were you trying to be a hero, or were you one of them?"

More silence.

"So what do you think now?" Bellar asked quietly, not sure if he wanted to hear the answer.

There was no answer. A burst of fire blew through the tree tops, lighting up Esaf's surprised face as it dropped upon him.

The heat blast threw Bellar backward, the salt pouch flying from his hands.

Esaf began screaming, just like the screams in Nedisse's stories. But it didn't last long. Bellar could see his friend within that strange undulating reddish glow as he withered and crisped. Just at that last instant before the spark of life fled, Esaf turned his eyes upon Bellar. In them, he read accusation. His friend's dead eyes said 'traitor'. Esaf thought he'd been led into a trap. He'd suspected it all along, Bellar realized; it was why Esaf had resisted entering the clearings.

Bellar tried to vomit, but could bring nothing up.

The viricama seemed to be savoring Esaf, making sounds that Bellar knew too well: the sounds of a woman enjoying sex, the sounds Uida made when her mouth—

His stomach heaved, but he felt dry on the inside. As he ran his hands through the grass, trying to find the lost salt pouch, he prayed to Kaja. He couldn't help

[57]

praying to her; he couldn't think of who else to pray to. He prayed that there was enough salt left, that he could find the third skin and salt it before he was burned. Even if he died, so would all the viricamas at sunrise.

Then he saw it. Another pile of skin tucked away at the base of a tree.

Searching, scrambling, the salt pouch eluded him but he got his hands on that pile of skin, on Uida. Her face, strangely, was beautiful even now in its flat lifelessness.

He stood, Uida's skin limp in his hands, her long black hair tickling his arms. The viricama hovered before him, its heat pleasant and comforting, like the nearby fire when he and Uida were sexing.

Did it know he had no salt left? When it did not attack, he knew that this viricama was Uida, and wondered if it had feelings for him.

He remembered Esaf's words, and read new meaning into them. If Uida were a viricama, what did that make him? If Esaf truly believed Bellar had destroyed the brine wells, perhaps others suspected the same. Perhaps Uida spared him now because the viricamas needed an ally...or a scapegoat. If Bellar returned from the vira alive, when none of the other men had, the tribe might suspect him of betrayal just as Esaf had.

He stared into the fireball, surprised it didn't hurt his eyes. He tried to see something of Uida in there, but there was nothing remotely human, nothing remotely woman.

And he had no salt, not even upon his skin for he was no longer sweating and could not feel the sting of salt on his skin. All salt — except that necessary to keep his body alive and functioning — had been drawn from him on purpose so that he could not even use his own salt to destroy her. But maybe there was just enough residue left....

Repulsed, yet craving the sensation of Uida's flesh against his, he rubbed her skin against him, the pliable mounds of her breasts soft against his chest and belly.

He felt only warmth, both from her skin and from the viricama, the warmth which Uida projected when she was amused with him. The fireball drifted closer; the heat — the heat between his legs — grew. Even now he could not deny the satisfaction an erection had always given him.

Uida wanted him, even in this form. He recognized it in the way a tongue of fire stretched out, not close enough to burn him, but enough to drive the erection to quickened hardness. Close enough to seem as if it was licking around his engorged penis as would Uida's tongue.

She could have it. He pulled at his breeches with one hand, yanking them down, and held her skin out with the other.

At first, the viricama ignored the offered skin. The tongue of fire flowed between his legs, as if it would embrace him. He sensed she wanted to sex him as a viricama, but when the fire briefly touched his penis he screamed — in pain and pleasure — and the fire tongue pulled back.

The fireball shimmered and began to dim, taking on human shape as it reached for the skin.

When Uida was half woman/half viricama, solid enough to touch, to penetrate, but still not fully within

[59]

her skin, he took her. He took the gamble that if there was enough salt left in him to keep him alive, there would still be salt in his semen. In her woman form, his semen had never harmed her, but maybe in this state when she was neither woman nor viricama, it would prevent her from fully reintegrating with her skin.

Too late she seemed to realize something was wrong and tried to pull free of her skin. But it was as if she were trapped as long as his penis was inside her, thrusting hard, thrusting to release. The fireball flared, fluctuating wildly, searing the skin around his groin, but he felt no pain.

Rather, Bellar had never known such pleasure. When he came it was like a star burst. Sparks showered his face in a firefly dance as the fireball silently exploded, then dimmed to nothingness. The last of Uida's juices —womanly or no—bathed him in such delicious warmth he just stood there still inside her empty skin until Kaja, in her nightly run through the sky, was overhead. He did not know if Kaja was laughing at him or blessing him.

Talebones

Finger bones and toe bones rattled inside the oracle's shaking fist, clacking and clinking as if the bones themselves were angry. When she opened her hand, the pieces fell from between her fingers like heavy raindrops in a thunderstorm. The bones hit the hard-packed dirt floor, bounced and bounced again, scattering in a seemingly random pattern, the last one landing in the bowl of holy water near her left hand. The surface of the water turned an oily gray, shielding the precious bone from view.

A hush fell over the petitioners. With a twisted frown on her wrinkled sun-darkened face, the oracle grabbed the bowl and flipped it upside down so quickly that no water splashed outside the circle it made on the dirt. Instead, the water trickled out from under the bowl in tiny rivulets toward the front row of people who scrambled up from their seated positions and away. Except Meela. She watched the slick water wind its way toward her via the scuff marks made by someone's toes to stop just inches from her fingertips. She dared not move, dared not lift her hands from their palm down position indicating her supplication.

Meela did lift her eyes to match the gaze of the oracle. The old woman's rheumy eyes didn't blink.

After a long moment, a relieved sigh ran through the tent—the only breath moving in the stifling, humid air. Meela relied on her ears to tell her when the other villagers began sitting down again, their thin cotton clothing rustling lightly, and her nose to tell her Jorad now sat directly behind her. The chief's son had not bathed in at least a week.

Everyone now sat behind her, as if Meela had been singled out by the oracle's strange powers. It wasn't an odd situation for Meela; she'd often felt alone or out of place in her birth village ever since she'd returned upon her mother's death a year ago. And that was why she sat here now, imploring the oracle for justice. Justice for her murdered mother.

"The bones do not lie." The oracle's strong voice belied her many years. "They are the purest parts of us, the strongest. When our voices have been silenced, only our bones can speak for us." The oracle had spoken these words many times and had mastered the technique of projecting her voice so it sounded like it was issuing from the scattered bones themselves. It never failed to impress the crowds, except for Meela who knew the secret to such petty tricks herself.

The last rays of the setting sun, peeking between ridges of the surrounding hills, burst through the unsecured tent flaps which fluttered in the suddenly rising breeze, shining upon the clean white bones. Showy, Meela thought. She'd not realized it as a child, but the oracle always held court when the late afternoon winds picked up and positioned the tent precisely to capture the sun's dying rays whatever the time of year.

For one horrible moment, Meela's faith in the oracle began to wane. The entertainer's tricks were simply a part of the ritual, weren't they? To silence the unbelievers. To reinforce the oracle's role as judge. It didn't mean all of the oracle's abilities were trickery. Meela's ability to read the flesh and blood of others certainly was no trick. The young, whose growing forms transmitted a mass of information, were especially easy to read, and adolescent bodies, with their rapid transformation from child to adult, shouted to Meela's senses so strongly she could smell them approaching before they came into sight. And young minds were as easy to read as young bodies.

Swaying with the breeze, the oracle held her arms in front of her, waving her hands over the bones. She closed her eyes, squeezing their milky yellow discharge out and down her cheeks like tears.

No one spoke. But from the stench of his farts, Meela knew Jorad was nervous. And well he should be. Passing by him and his father every day during her trips to the central well, knowing what they had done to her mother, had been too much for her. In her anger and hatred, she'd threatened him, privately, and then gone looking for her mother's bones in the rice paddies which should have been Meela's inheritance.

Justice for Meela's mother would have to wait just a little longer though, as the oracle's hand paused over the tiniest bones in the collection. No one had to ask to whom they belonged: frail Emina, newborn of Dorag and Yuseela. Rumor had it that Yuseela had shaken the baby too hard or that Dorag had stepped on his own daughter after too much rice wine.

Truthfully, frail Emina's blood was bad and would have killed her before her first birthday if her oldest sister hadn't smothered her. But only Meela knew that. It was Meela who'd put the thought in the sister's head. For Meela, who'd seen a child die of the disease in her husband's village, it was a mercy killing...and a means to bring the number of dead seeking justice to three, a requirement for the oracle's ministrations.

[63]

The oracle panted rapidly, almost like a woman in labor. Her arms became rigid, stringy old muscles standing out in stark relief against the old woman's papery skin. Her fingers curled in, trembling as if resisting a force pulling them in tighter. The joint disease, Meela told herself. The oracle was creatively using her age-related infirmities as part of the act.

After what seemed an eternity, the oracle snatched up one of the bone fragments and flung it into the crowd all without ever opening her eyes.

Meela watched over her shoulder as the bone flew past Jorad, past Dorag and Yuseela, past crazy Ulenny, and struck Esana—Emina's oldest sister—in the forehead.

Esana's eyes, squeezed shut like the oracle's, flew open. Her young fair skin burned a bright red. The fourteen year old girl burst into tears.

The dead baby's parents gasped, in horror and relief.

Jorad motioned to his younger brothers, not that much older than Esana, who grabbed the girl by her arms and dragged her from the darkening tent. She whimpered protests, but no one listened. No one spoke on her behalf. The bones had spoken.

Yuseela and Dorag wept quietly, but Meela could still see the relief on their faces. They'd been cleared of suspicion, spared watching their baby die, and—although they didn't know it—spared from the exorbitant dowry marrying off a barren daughter like Esana would have cost them. With as little as Yuseela and Dorag had, they would've been forced to sell their land to compensate Esana's outraged future husband, leaving no inheritance for their sons. To Meela it was a mercy killing too.

And it was all proof that the oracle's powers were true. There was no other way for her to identify Esana as the killer—Meela had seen to that—except for the bones to tell her.

Now, would it next be Meela seeing justice done for her mother, or would it be old man Poley—the third petitioner—who insisted it was the jealous daughter-in-law who killed his wife, not he?

The oracle went back into her act. Her hands wavered over the scattered bones as if she couldn't tell whose were whose. Suddenly she leaned forward, her own bones creaking in protest, and picked up the overturned bowl with one hand and grabbed the hidden bone with the other. Meela caught only the briefest of glimpses of the bone—turned a sickening blackish color—before it struck her in the forehead.

Even Jorad gasped. Then laughed.

Meela was certain her face was as red as Esana's had been, but hers was not shame.

The oracle blinked at her as if trying to remember who she was.

Jorad motioned to his younger brothers who were just reentering the tent.

Meela stood up. "I did not murder my mother!" She pointed to Jorad, still sitting cross-legged behind her. "He did!"

"The bones never miss," the oracle said. Heads nodded. They'd all seen it themselves, bones bouncing off dirt or a tent pole or a hearthstone in order to strike murdering cowards hiding behind innocent people.

She shrugged off Jorad's brothers. "I did not murder her! You all know I was living in my husband's village on the other side of the Tarek Mountains when she died."

"We know no such thing," Jorad spoke for the first time. His voice was infuriatingly deep, entrancing, stimulating. "Your husband's village cast you out with charges of witchcraft." He shrugged as he slowly stood up to look her in the eyes. Tall for a woman, Meela matched him inch for inch. "They had no proof they could share, but they wanted no part of you nor any offspring you might produce. You've been wandering the hills for nearly two years now, time enough to plot the death of your mother and, with no living brothers, to take over her land holdings. It was the only way for you ever to gain a home again."

Meela's mother had married well, and with the loss of husband and sons, had come into possession of the village's largest and best rice paddies, twice as much as the chief's family. More than enough to generate jealousy and greed.

"That is why you killed her," Meela said in a low voice. "Her land." All the while they spoke, she worked at his mind, trying to undo its folds, to rearrange them. But it was useless. She could picture his brain, its intricate pulsating ridges, but couldn't pull them apart. They were packed too tightly together. It had always been this way, the older a person the less effect she had on their thoughts, as if their brains developed an immunity to her powers with all that muscle mass folding in on itself as it matured and tucked away memories and lessons, hiding away the vulnerable spots that her thoughts were otherwise able to influence.

The only adult mind she'd ever been able to touch was Nahmia's, her own mother, and even then all Meela received were images and emotions: like Jorad's face and hands as he stabbed Nahmia in the gut, like panic as Jorad threw Nahmia into the rice paddy before she was even dead. The terror of drowning.

Jorad's face rippled, as if Meela were looking at him from below the red-tinged water's surface—her mother's last vision. "Your family's power is waning. You needed my mother's land to solidify your hold on the village or else your son would never have the stature to become chief when he is of age."

Jorad stepped closer, pressing up against her, as his brothers grabbed her arms to hold her in place. To her disgust, she could feel herself trembling, not just with fear, but with revulsion at the thrust of his hardened penis against her. If they'd been unclothed, he would've penetrated her.

Softly, so no one else could hear, he said, "If you were not a witch, I'd have you simply for the pleasure of teaching you a lesson."

She spat in his face. "You murdered my mother."

"The bones do not lie," the oracle pronounced.

Meela turned her head to glare at the old woman. "How did they buy your trickery?"

"You are the trickster," the old woman said as she rose. She stepped carefully over the bone fragments and stood on her tiptoes so she could whisper into Meela's ear. "Playing with the minds of children."

Meela's heart thudded against her chest.

"That was not one of your mother's bones I threw," the oracle whispered more, "It was another of Emina's."

"She would've died horribly anyway. I've seen it."

"So have I." The oracle "tsk"ed under her breath. "You are an amateur, my dear foolish Meela. If perhaps you'd been born to me, I could've taught you real gifts."

"What could I have learned from a liar and a thief?"

The oracle shrugged. "Survival."

Meela looked at the other villagers, who'd scurried to huddle in the back of the tent at the first mention of witchcraft. They'd heard none of the exchange. "Jorad murdered my mother for her land! I only came to seek justice for her!" She had no proof of her vision, no way to explain how she knew without labeling herself a witch, without ruining any chance she had for vengeance. The others must believe her innocent or they wouldn't believe her bones.

"No, you are the murderer we have sought." Jorad smiled, but none of the others could see it. "Finally your mother's soul can rest."

No one contradicted him. No one spoke on her behalf.

She spat in his face, satisfied how the spittle streaked his lips and at his revulsion. If he truly believed in her powers, he might think he was now cursed.

As it had been in her husband's village, the others simply watched her being dragged away, this time to her death.

Amateur, the oracle had called her. Well, the old woman would see the truth for herself. In Meela's own experiments with bones, she'd discovered she could not affect those of others, but could feel strange things happening to her own bones. If she turned her mind inward to the folds of her own brain, to the folds of her muscles and sinew, to the traces of her blood vessels, she could see all that happened within her own body. At first a chilling experience, but now a means of revenge.

As Jorad's brothers took her out to the village midden and placed her face down over the chopping block, she burst tiny blood vessels inside her legs, and used the hot pulsing liquid to write on the long bones the names of her mother's murderers—now her murderers—the oracle included. Over and over again, she burnt the red letters into the white bones, so there would be no mistakes, no mischance should one of the mangy mutts who scavenged for food in the midden run off with a limb.

Jorad's youngest brother raised the axe.

Justice for her mother, her bones asked for. And bones do not lie, the oracle said it herself. It would be many days before her bones could speak for her, but to bones time is of little importance, only the stories they can—

In the Service of the Queen

First, Paolo died, then Francois and Jean-Pierre, and then Mario and Marcel...the list went on. Of the twenty-member Queen's Guard, only three remained. Emile, Gino and Luc stood in the dusty roadway, surrounding the horse-drawn wagon holding the queen's bier. Spindly creatures, resembling giant sloths with porcupine quills instead of fur, dropped from the surrounding trees. They were easily the height of two men, but Emile doubted they weighed even half of what he did without armor.

"Maybe they don't want her back," Gino sniped under his breath. It was not the first time he'd made such a suggestion.

This time Emile did not spare a rebuke or even a glance at his subordinate. His eye was better kept on these fast-moving arboreals and the thick, but sharp claws on each hand and foot. Consciously keeping his hand away from his sword, he straightened his road-worn uniform tunic and gave a slight bow, hoping they understood human gestures and languages.

"We wish you no harm. We only want to pass through your woods to the Huikugy city."

When the creature nearest him spoke, it was like words being drowned inside a cat's purr. "We guard the Huikugy against their enemies."

Emile could see nothing that resembled a weapon on any of the creatures — now numbering six — except their claws. Those claws dug into the dirt as each creature settled on its haunches. Their stance seemed to indicate relaxation, but the way the quills stood up stiffly — like hundreds of needles — warned Emile otherwise.

"We are not their enemies. I am Captain Emile Diallo of the Queen's Guard. We bring home the Huikugy queen."

"The queen is safe inside her fortress."

"This is Aulifarwoon, the daughter of Asalioral, the ancestor of your present king. She was married to our king of Madri." Purely a political liaison because the Huikugy were not remotely human.

The alliance had gained exactly what the humans wanted, a friendly neighbor on its western border, but little else. The Huikugy were notoriously isolationist — even more so than the Torumbur to the north — but still were capable of preventing incursions into Madri by the warlike Arijia.

A rumbling purr passed through the assembled creatures as they glanced at one another, their small black eyes unreadable.

"They don't understand," Luc said softly.

It wasn't surprising that the creatures didn't know of what Emile spoke. The Huikugy were quite long-lived compared to other species. These creatures probably weren't born before this queen left Huikugy lands. Likewise, the original Madri king to whom she'd initially been wed had died over a century ago. His successors had inherited their foreign queen at ascension. And Emile was not the first captain of her guard.

"No human may pass, by order of the king."

"The treaty—"

"—has been nullified by King Revasnatir."

"When?"

"One moon ago."

Emile shared an uneasy look with the other two men. The queen's guard had left Madera, the capital of Madri, in the Boralle Province, twenty-eight days ago immediately upon the queen's passing. How could the Huikugy have known? There'd been no way to notify them...unless the rumors about Huikugy mental powers were true. Emile didn't believe those rumors — he'd sensed nothing from his enigmatic queen — and didn't believe anyway that the queen's death would affect the treaty even if the Huikugy already knew. She had died of natural causes, old age; her human subjects had played no part in it. Emile could personally assure the Huikugy of that.

The creatures had not moved.

"We bring the queen home so she may be buried among her own kind, in her homeland."

The queen had left no instructions for the treatment of her remains. As it was the human custom that the dead must be buried in his or her birthplace — even if it meant relatives must take on an arduous journey — the widowed king decreed Queen Aulifarwoon be returned to her people.

The rumbling purr increased in intensity; Emile could almost feel it through his thick boots.

He tried a new tact. "If I may be so bold to ask, perhaps you could escort us to the city gate." He could suggest these creatures take the queen for the rest of her final journey, but he wouldn't do that. Not only did honor dictate he remain with his queen, but he had no way of knowing if these creatures truly guarded the city at the behest of the Huikugy.

"This queen you speak of is dead?"

Gino stifled an incredulous laugh, but only after Emile glared at him.

What did these creatures think was beneath the dirty tarp on the wagon? Its shape — squat, round, with eight limbs – was obviously an Huikugy body. Not to mention the smell. Emile had grown immune to it, but not even their best doctors could develop a preservative to keep the body from decaying for a month.

The creatures' purr evolved into a growl. "No. Touching the dead is forbidden."

The creatures surged forward. Emile focused upon the claw on the end of the lanky arm swinging at him as he drew his sword. But it was the quills he should've watched for. The claw clanged harmlessly against the metal sword; when the creature drew its arm back, the quills raked along his sleeve, piercing the fabric and the skin. It was like having fire poured into his flesh through open wounds. Sparks flitted between the ends of the broken-off quills, setting fire to the fabric.

The creature swung with its other arm; Emile — the closest of the three men to the two horses — ducked under the nearest horse while he clawed at the sleeve, ripping off the burning portion, and furiously plucking at the quills. A second creature lunged at him from the opposite side. Instead of the man, their quills struck the horses.

As the horses bucked and fought their harnesses, screaming wildly, Emile dropped into a fetal position, his hands protecting his head. The stench of burning horseflesh overpowered everything, even the stench of the dead queen.

He could hear Gino screaming too, or maybe it was Luc.

A kick from a hoof knocked the breath out of him, and then a wagon wheel ran over his left foot as the crazed horses, trying to escape the pain and the flames, surged forward. Kicking and stomping, the horses trampled right over the two creatures trying to reach Emile. Viscous, orange blood spurted from the dead creatures' wounds, running in rivulets through the dirt, bursting into flames wherever it happened to cross a fallen quill.

Their path now free of obstacles, the horses ran, the wagon lumbering awkwardly behind them, its wheels bouncing. The bier, jostled about, slid dangerously close to the wagon's edge just as the horses rounded a curve in the road. The only sign of their whereabouts were puffs of smoke drifting over the treetops.

Still trying to catch a breath, Emile grabbed his dropped sword and dipped it into the burning liquid. Its viscousness made it stick to the metal well. Flaming sword in hand, he turned to help his men.

Luc lay on the ground, his uniform smoking. Two dead creatures sprawled nearby, their severed arms making a neat frame around the downed man. Despite the evidence, Emile knew Luc had not killed them himself. Luc was the worst swordsmen in the Queen's Guard which, ironically, had saved his life until now because the other men took it upon themselves to make up for his weakness and protected him.

Gino, who was the best swordsman in the guard, parried the swinging arms of a third creature. Its quills made strange twanging sounds as they broke off against the metal. Smoke rose between the pair, but Emile couldn't see who or what burned.

A fourth creature, severely wounded, struggled to its feet and lumbered toward Emile. Immune to its own blood, it stepped right through the burning liquid. Emile nearly faltered seeing that — his only idea hinged upon his flaming sword — but he had to try. He leapt forward, into the creature's reach, and nearly fell down when his left foot folded under him. The wheel running over it must have broken one or more of its many bones.

Ignoring the pain, he planted his feet firmly in a rut in the road, and ran his sword into the creature's chest. It almost didn't penetrate so tough was the creature's skin, and when it punched through Emile stumbled forward nearly getting his face splattered by gushing blood.

As he hoped, only the creature's hide was immune to the blood. It was like setting fire to fire. The creature made an "urp" sound, its chest glowing from the inside. And then it burst open, like an exploding fireplace Emile had encountered as a child. Flaming innards showered Emile, who dropped and rolled to snuff out flames licking at his uniform.

When he stood again, the remaining creature was down, but so was Gino.

Emile patted out the flames eating away at Gino's torso. His maroon tunic had been burned away, except for the back and upper sleeves where the insignia of Queen Aulifarwoon's protectors was sewn on.

Designed by Emile's great-great-great grandfather, it was a simple eight-pointed star.

Gino coughed. "Luc?"

Emile checked the other man and shook his head.

Gino swore under his breath. "I promised Luc's father we'd keep the cub alive on this journey." He coughed again; this time blood came up.

Emile didn't try to fight off a smile. As captain, he too often indulged Gino's improprieties, such as giving diminutive nicknames to Luc, but now was not the time to reprimand him.

"I've been insolent again, haven't I?" Gino sounded only partially contrite. "Forgive me, my captain."

"You've always been insolent." It wasn't a condemnation.

"You'll have to—" he gasped, "to leave us here."

Emile shook his head. "No. I'll not leave your body in a foreign land. You will be buried amongst your ancestors as you should be."

"You can't carry..."

...two of us, Emile finished the thought. "I will."

Each dead man had been taken home by another, reducing their ranks. Carmine had to be assigned to take both Mario's and Marcel's bodies home because no more men could be spared. These decisions made the queen's guard more vulnerable, but Emile could not break tradition nor disappoint the families of his guardsmen. And now he most certainly could not risk losing the souls of his dead subordinates to foreigners' witchcraft; should the Arijia discover the treaty's dissolution, their reputed magicians might soon be swarming through these lands.

That left to Emile the task of taking home both Luc and Gino. But first, his queen.

"I will come back for you. Perhaps we're not that far from the city."

Gino gave him a blood-rimmed smile. "The queen's man to the last. Did she ever appreciate you enough?"

Emile couldn't answer that question. Not only had his queen never spoken directly to him, or shown any emotion toward him, but Gino was now dead. The question was pointless.

He would see his queen home, and then he'd take his men back to their home in Boralle. He left Gino and Luc where they lay knowing any more of those creatures who might happen along would not touch the dead. But he would have to worry about more creatures.

He collected all three swords, but then had a better idea. He sliced away the skin of one of the creatures — a tough job; it was like sawing tree bark with a dagger. The task left him even more out of breath then the fight had. And it dulled two of the swords, which he left lying in the bloody road.

Careful to touch only a patch devoid of quills and blood, he dragged the skin along behind him as he limped down the road. He'd see if the creatures wouldn't touch even their own dead.

The horses could not have gone far, not before the fire killed them. As expected, not even a half mile down around the curve of the road, the queen's bier lay in the dirt. The tarp still covered her body, but several of her legs could be seen. Queen Aulifarwoon had claws for feet and scales instead of skin.

The wagon lay, overturned, against a tree trunk, its baseboards and wheels shattered. The wagon's other contents — their supplies — were scattered about. The horses lay, smoke rising from their charred corpses, just a bit further along.

What Emile didn't expect was how close to the city they'd actually been. From where he stood, the road rose up a slight hill to where wooden gates stood closed at the crest. But he couldn't see any signs of a city, only more trees and the tops of what looked like large dirt mounds. Somehow, despite the physical differences between humans and Huikugy, he had expected something resembling human-built structures. His queen had adapted well enough to Madera.

He also saw no sign of habitation except for three sloth-like creatures hanging from tree branches on either side of him. When he brandished the hide of their dead compatriot, they hissed at him, but did not approach.

He covered up his dead queen, and began gathering unburned rope from their supplies to turn the bier into a sled. He'd have to drag her to the city gates which he suspected might be merely an affectation the Huikugy put up to satisfy the expectations of foreigners.

He found himself increasingly short of breath as he worked, accompanied by a sharp pain in his chest. Emile worried the horse kick had done significant damage, but pushed it from his mind. He must deliver his queen to her own people.

But the Huikugy came to him. Perhaps alerted by more sloth-like creatures he couldn't see, or those rumored mental powers, the gates creaked open and out scurried a half-dozen Huikugy.

His human preconceptions again betrayed him. He expected that intelligent, civilization-building creatures would look as different from one another as humans did, but he would not have been able to identify his own queen if she stood alive today amongst her kin.

The Huikugy were squat, rounded somewhat like tortoises, with dark gray scales, and eight legs like arachnids. Their necks and heads, covered by light gray feathers, were avian except for the near-human-like mouth where a beak might be expected.

They did not speak to him, not with those mouths. Their words hammered inside his head, drowning out the pain in his chest.

"Human, human, human...."

By reflex, he clapped his hands over his ears even though it didn't help.

"Human, human, human...."

"I brought her home to you!" he yelled. "The daughter of King Asalioral." His words echoed amongst the trees, seeming to startle the Huikugy.

"Human, human, human... this is a carcass, carcass, carcass...."

"It is Queen Aulifarwoon! Daughter of King Asalioral."

"Carcass, carcass, carcass...."

Finally one voice broke in over the mental echoes. "Did you learn nothing from her reign amongst your people? Humans had over a century of your time to learn about the Huikugy."

"What?"

"Did you not recognize she was dying?"

"Yes, but our doctors didn't know what to do. She was just old, they said."

"Irrelevant, irrelevant, irrelevant...."

"We care not for carcasses, only the souls. You should have brought her back before her body died, before her soul was lost forever amongst your foreign souls."

So similar to the thought he'd had about his own men's souls. But did Huikugy have souls like humans did?

"She did not tell us."

"She should not have had to. You should have learned."

"I spent every waking moment with the queen. She taught me nothing except how well she had adapted to living among humans." Perhaps Queen Aulifarwoon had been too human in her manners by the time Emile came into her service. Her own ways so alien to her that she no longer could share them with her new guards.

Perhaps she had become so human she should have been buried in Madera.

The thought tore through him, the anguish more painful than the cough racking his chest. He stared, bleakly, at the pink spittle on his hands. The horse's kick — broken ribs, punctured lung....

"Please, my duty is to return her to you for burial. I must see my duty finished. It is all I ask."

"Too late, too late, too late...."

"Please. I've pledged my life to her, my life and the life of my men to bring her back."

"And your life you've given."

One of the Huikugy scuttled closer and cocked its head to one side so it could look him in the eyes. He'd always been fascinated by the multifaceted, multicolored Huikugy eyes.

"Be satisfied, human, that you brought her to our gate."

"What will you do with her?" He coughed more blood.

"We do nothing with carcasses. She will lay here until the carrion-eaters are finished with her." The Huikugy let out a brief whistling breath — the equivalent of a sigh. "You completed your duty. Be content."

"I have not."

"You have."

"I must take my men home to be buried with our kind."

"You die before us now. Once you are a carcass, we can not touch you." Another short whistling breath. "You will lie here with your queen."

Until the carrion-eaters picked his bones cleaned.

"I promised—"

"Humans have made many promises."

"Promises, promises, promises..." echoed in his head.

"Promises made without understanding. We have lost as much as you. We will never be complete again because Aulifarwoon's soul is lost to us. You failed your queen's soul."

"Soul, soul, soul...."

How could the Huikugy belief in a soul be so human-like when the two species were so different? He'd never considered his queen's soul. He protected her — her body — from narrow-minded humans who resented an alien in their royal household.

"Soul, soul, soul...."

No matter how many times he had stared into his queen's eyes, he'd seen no hint of a soul there, only bizarrely distorted reflections of himself.

"I have not failed," Emile insisted. "I brought her home." He couldn't have failed. Failed to learn the most fundamental aspect of the queen he served. Failed to learn how to read those eyes, her thoughts. Failed to learn the one thing humans and Huikugy shared.

"I have not failed," he said again. He had pledged to bring her body home; he'd done that. Her body was his responsibility, not her soul.

"As you wish it."

"I have not failed. I brought her home." He couldn't remember if he was repeating himself.

The Huikugy said nothing more, even the echoes died away as they scurried back inside their gate.

"I have not failed," Emile repeated to himself as he lay down in the road next to his queen.

About the Authors

Xina Marie Uhl lives in sunny Southern California with her husband and assorted furry and scaly pets. The setting of her first novel, *Necropolis*, along with much of her other writing, has been heavily influenced by her interest in ancient history. She holds both a BA and an MA in history. In addition to fiction writing, she teaches history and writes educational materials. When she isn't reading and writing, she enjoys hiking, photography, and planning new travel adventures. She maintains a blog at xuwriter.wordpress.com.

Xina's available ebooks include:

Necropolis

The Gauntlet Thrown and *The Challenge Accepted* (with Cheryl Dyson)

A Fairy Tail and Out of the Bag

The Cat's Guide to Human Behavior

She also maintains a web presence on Facebook (www.facebook.com/XinaMarieUhl) and Twitter (www.twitter.com/xuwriter)

Born and raised in the Midwest, **Janet Loftis** fled to sunny California to escape the cold, dark winters, only to now explore the colder and darker sides of human nature in her horror and fantasy fiction.

With a BA in Anthropology and Archaeology, and a MA combining Cultural Anthropology with Creative

Writing, Janet's stories are inspired by the mythos of cultures around the world. From science-fiction to fantasy to horror, and from short stories to screenplays, Janet has seen her fiction published in a variety of online and print magazines, and placed in the finals and semi-finals of screenplay competitions.

Next on Janet's agenda are more horror shorts, a horror screenplay, and the marketing of a family-friendly screenplay.

The three stories published here are taken from *Skin and Bones*, a collection of eleven short stories and a novelette currently available from XC Publishing.net. These dark-tinged, anthropology-inspired tales will intrigue fans of horror, dark fantasy, magical realism, and science fiction.

More short story collections by Janet L. Loftis:

Zombies And Aliens

Ivy League

The Box Quadrilogy

Wheels and Deals

Connect with Janet online:

Facebook (www.Facebook.com/JanetLoftis)

Amazon Author Page

(www.Amazon.com/author/JanetLoftis)

Follow her blog The Far Places (janetloftis.wordpress.com) exploring creativity, travel and cats.

A Request of the Reader ...

If you enjoyed this book, please consider helping the authors by leaving a review of it. Even very short reviews are cherished!

www.ingramcontent.com/pod-product-compliance
Lightning Source LLC
Chambersburg PA
CBHW070607180626
46817CB00005B/2033